Gwen
the
Beauty and the Beast Fairy

Special thanks to Tracey West

ISBN 978-0-545-88740-3

10 9 8 7 6 5 4   16 17 18 19 20

Printed in the U.S.A.   40

First edition, January 2016

Gwen

the
Beauty and the
Beast Fairy

by Daisy Meadows

SCHOLASTIC INC.

Jack Frost's
Ice Castle

Forest

Tiptop Castle

The Fairy Tale Fairies are in for a shock!
Cinderella won't run at the strike of the clock.
No one can stop me—I've plotted and planned,
And I'll be the fairest one in all of the land.

It will take someone handsome and witty and clever
To stop storybook endings forever and ever.
But to see fairies suffer great trouble and strife,
Will make me live happily all of my life!

Contents

Fairy Tale Creatures

"When I get back home, I'm going to try to make some of this fairy tale food," Kirsty Tate said. "These Peter Pancakes are delicious!"

"And so is this Fairyland Fruit Salad," agreed her friend, Rachel Walker.

The two girls were in the big dining room at Tiptop Castle. The tables were

filled with boys and girls who had come
for the Fairy Tale Festival. Each day, the
festival organizers had fun activities
planned for them.

Just being in the castle was like living
inside a fairy tale. The meals were served
on pretty silver plates, and all the food
had a fairy tale theme. The Peter
Pancakes were shaped like fairy wings.
The Fairyland Fruit Salad came in a

crystal goblet
with a tall stem.
Kirsty sighed.
"I wish this
festival never
had to end," she
said, taking
another bite of
pancake.

A hush came over the room as Amy, one of the organizers, stood up. She was dressed as a princess in a pink dress with a pointy pink hat on top of her blond curls.

"Good morning, fairy tale fans!" she began. "We have a very exciting event planned tonight. It's the Creature Costume Party!"

The kids all began to whisper excitedly.

"There are many marvelous creatures in fairy tales," Amy said. "Unicorns, dragons, talking bears—the possibilities are endless. We have set up the ballroom with all the supplies you will need to make your costumes for tonight. So have fun, and use your imaginations. There will be prizes for the best costumes!"

Kirsty turned to Rachel. "It's fun that we get to make our own costumes!"

Rachel nodded. "I know. What do you think we should be?"

"I don't know." Kirsty frowned. "A unicorn would be fun."

"I bet a lot of people are going to be unicorns," said Rachel, looking thoughtful. "To win a prize, we should be something really different. Like a . . . a griffin!"

"What's a griffin?" asked Kirsty.

"It's a half-lion, half-eagle," Rachel said.

"A griffin sounds interesting," Kirsty agreed. "Or maybe we could be some kind of sea serpent!"

"We should look at the fairy tale books in the reading room," Rachel suggested. "I'm sure we'll find some good ideas there."

"That sounds like a great plan," Kirsty said.

Then Rachel looked around the dining room. She lowered her voice so only Kirsty could hear her. "Besides making our costumes for the party tonight, we also need to keep an eye out for the Fairy Tale Fairies."

"And for mean Jack Frost," Kirsty added.

Kirsty and Rachel were friends with the fairies in Fairyland. On their first day at Tiptop Castle, Hannah the Happily Ever After Fairy had come to see them. She took them to Fairy Tale Lane in Fairyland.

There they learned that Jack Frost was causing trouble again. He had stolen the magic object belonging to each of the Fairy Tale Fairies! Jack Frost wanted the fairy tales to be all about him.

Now the fairy tale characters were missing from their stories. Kirsty and Rachel had helped the Fairy Tale Fairies find four magic objects so far. But they still had three more objects to find—and three fairy tales to save.

"So far, every character we've met

has been somewhere in the castle,"
Rachel said.

"Or on the grounds," Kirsty added.
"The Frog Princess was hopping across
the lawn."

"And Jack Frost was nearby every
time!" Rachel said.

The girls finished breakfast and left the
dining room. They walked through
the grand entrance hall. A glittering
chandelier shimmered over their heads.
In front of them, two suits of armor stood
guard in front of a wide staircase.

Rachel was about to open the door to
the reading room when Kirsty nudged her.

"Rachel, look!"

A tall man came down the staircase.
He wore a fancy blue velvet suit and a

shirt with a ruffled collar. But his hands and face were covered in brown fur! He had pointy ears, a black nose, and tusks, too.

"That must be one of the fairy tale organizers," Rachel guessed. "He's dressed like Beast from *Beauty and the Beast.*"

Then they heard the sound of tinkling bells. The doorknob Rachel had just been holding shimmered with fairy magic. When the magic settled, a tiny fairy was perched there.

"That *is* the Beast!" she cried.

The Missing Pin

"Quick! In here!" Kirsty whispered.

The fairy followed the girls as they ducked into the reading room. The Fairy Tale Festival was full of amazing sights. But Kirsty and Rachel would have a hard time explaining to everyone that they knew a real fairy!

"Hello again, Kirsty and Rachel," the fairy said. "I'm Gwen the Beauty and the Beast Fairy. I met you on Fairy Tale Lane."

Auburn curls bounced off her shoulders. She wore a pretty blue skirt with white polka dots and a white blouse with a skinny blue ribbon around the collar. A bright yellow cardigan sweater topped off the outfit.

"If that is the Beast out there, that means that Jack Frost is up to no good," Rachel said.

Gwen nodded. "Jack Frost has my magic rose pin," the fairy explained. "Without it, I can't control the Beauty

and the Beast fairy tale. So that's why
the Beast is wandering around this
castle. He is lost and very confused."

"Poor Beast!" Kirsty said.

"Did somebody say Beast?" asked a
voice behind them.

The girls turned around. A young
woman was standing by one
of the tall bookshelves. She
wore a long, pale blue
skirt that touched her
brown boots, and a
white blouse with puffy
sleeves. Her big, dark
eyes looked worried.
"Is your name Beauty?"
Rachel asked.

The woman nodded.
She gazed at all the

books, which were stacked up to the ceiling. "I am looking for a magical book that my friend Beast gave me," she said. "One moment I had it, and the next moment, I didn't. It must be in here somewhere. But this doesn't look like Beast's library at all."

"We have to help her!" Kirsty whispered to Gwen and Rachel.

"The best way to help her is to find my missing rose pin," replied Gwen. "That is the only way to get her and Beast back to their fairy tale."

"We have to find Jack Frost," Rachel whispered.

Beauty ran to another of the tall bookshelves. "I must find my book!" she muttered to herself.

"What book is she looking for?" Kirsty asked.

"In the fairy tale, Beast gives Beauty a magical book," Gwen explained. "When she reads from it, the book will grant any wish she wants."

"That's right!" said Rachel. "I remember reading that in the story."

Kirsty shuddered. "Imagine what Jack Frost would do if he had that book. He would probably wish to rule all of Fairyland!"

Rachel's blue eyes went wide. "Oh no! What if he already has the book?"

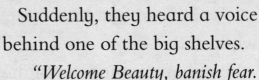

Suddenly, they heard a voice behind one of the big shelves.

"Welcome Beauty, banish fear.
You are the real princess here.
Speak your wishes, loud
and true.
And this book will obey you."

Gwen's wings fluttered. "I know that voice! That's Beauty's book speaking!"

Come to Me!

The girls raced toward the sound of the voice. Gwen flew above their heads. They turned a corner and there was Jack Frost!

Jack Frost hadn't seen them yet. Gwen motioned the girls to hide behind a bookshelf.

"Okay, book, I'm going to speak my wishes," Jack Frost was saying to the

thick book. It had a leather cover
decorated with flowers and leaves.

The girls noticed Gwen's pin glittering
on Jack Frost's shirtfront.

"There it is!" Gwen
whispered.

Then they heard
the book speak.
"Wait, you're not
Beauty! Good-bye
and go away!" it
said. And then
it slammed shut!

"But I *am* Beauty! This is *my* fairy tale
now!" Jack Frost cried. He angrily
stomped his foot.

Just then, the real Beauty ran up the
aisle toward Jack Frost. Before the girls
or Gwen could do anything, she reached

out to grab the book. "That's mine!
Beast gave it to me. What are you doing
with it?" she asked Jack Frost.

Jack Frost scowled. "No way! It's mine
now!" he yelled, clutching
the book to his chest.
With a flash of light
and a cloud of icy
magic, Jack Frost
disappeared from
the library.

"No!"
Beauty
yelled. "Oh
dear. I must find
Beast!" Beauty turned and hurried out
of the library.

"Poor Beauty." Gwen looked
distraught. "I'm going to follow her and

make sure she's okay. You girls keep an
eye out for Jack Frost," she told them.
"I'm sure he's still somewhere in the
castle."

"We'll look everywhere for him!"
Kirsty promised as Gwen fluttered away.

"We should start inside the castle, and
then go outside," Rachel suggested.

The girls quickly began their search.
Downstairs, they looked in the dining
room, the ballroom, and the kitchen.
Then they went upstairs and walked up
and down every hallway looking for
him. Finally, they climbed the castle's
tall turrets.

Rachel gazed out the window at the
castle grounds below.

"He could be anywhere," she said with
a sigh.

"We've got to keep looking," said
Kirsty. "Think of poor Beauty and the
Beast, lost outside their fairy tale!"

Rachel nodded. "Let's go."

They ran all the way downstairs and
began searching the castle grounds. First,
they looked in the courtyard. The water in
the shell-shaped fountain bubbled happily,
but there was no sign of Jack Frost.

They walked over the moat, but
they didn't see Jack Frost there,
either. They walked through the rose
garden. They saw Beauty happily
smelling the roses, but there was no sign
of Jack Frost.

Kirsty spotted
Gwen hiding in
a rose bloom.
"I think
Beauty's
okay for
now," she
said. "But the
sooner we get
my magic rose
pin back, the better!"
The girls nodded. Gwen tucked herself
into Rachel's pocket so they could

continue their search without anyone
spotting her.

Then the sound of a bell rang across
the castle grounds.

"Is it time for lunch already?" asked
Rachel.

"We've been looking for Jack Frost
all morning!" said Kirsty. She
patted her stomach. "I guess I
am pretty hungry."

"The organizers will be
worried if we don't show up,"
Rachel said. "Let's eat fast
and keep looking for the
rose pin."

The girls went back inside
the castle and quickly ate their
lunch of Princess Pasta Salad
and cucumber sandwiches cut

into crown shapes. Gwen kept out of sight in Rachel's pocket.

As they ate, Rachel and Kirsty noticed the other kids at their table were talking about the costumes they were making. Some of them had paint streaks on their faces and glitter on their clothes.

"We have been so busy looking for Jack Frost, we forgot about our creature costumes!" said Kirsty.

Rachel looked thoughtful. "Well, we've looked everywhere we can. I think we can probably start our costumes after lunch. Besides, Jack Frost usually turns up when we least expect him, anyway!"

Kirsty nodded. "That's for sure."

"I hope you're right, girls," Gwen whispered. "If he doesn't show up soon, we might have to visit his Ice Castle."

She shuddered. No fairy was a fan of his frozen palace.

The girls finished lunch and headed for the ballroom. Tables had been set up with all kinds of craft supplies: felt, fake fur, feathers, glue, pom-poms, and more. Groups of kids crowded around the supplies, or spread their work-in-progress costumes on the floor.

Kirsty's eyes went wide. "I think everything in the craft store is here!"

"We should look around," said Rachel. "Maybe we'll get an idea for our costumes."

As they approached the tables, they heard a loud, demanding voice coming from a corner of the room.

"Obey me, book! I am Beauty!"

"I know that voice!" Kirsty cried.

None other than Jack Frost stood behind one of the craft tables in a corner of the ballroom. He was angrily shaking Beauty's book. Gwen's magic rose pin still glittered on his shirt. Even though Jack Frost was being loud, no one was paying much attention to him.

"Everyone must think he's practicing his fairy tale character for the ball tonight," Rachel guessed. "Let's sneak over there and see what he's up to."

"Be careful girls," Gwen whispered.

Kirsty and Rachel ducked behind the table next to Jack Frost. He slammed down the book and frowned.

"If this book won't make my wishes come true, then my goblins will!" he cried. He clapped his hands, motioning four green goblins toward him. The goblins were all dressed as fairy tale animals, so the girls hadn't immediately noticed them in the crowd of kids. One was dressed as a bear, one as a cat, one as a wolf, and one as a mouse.

"I want to use all this stuff to make a beautiful princess dress. Once I'm dressed

like Beauty, this book will have to obey me!" said Jack Frost. "I need some glitter. Glitter, come to me!"

The goblins looked at one another and scratched their heads.

"I want the glitter to *magically* come to me," Jack Frost growled. "That means one of you needs to go get it for me!"

The goblin dressed as a cat nodded and ran to find glitter. He knocked over a

box of feathers in the process, and they flew all over the ballroom.

"Yarn, come to me!" Jack Frost yelled, and the goblin dressed as a bear leaped up, looking for yarn. He ran up to a boy holding a ball of green yarn and grabbed it right out of his hands.

"Hey!" cried the boy.

"Feathers, come to me! Ribbons, come to me!" Jack Frost yelled, and the other two goblins jumped into action.

The one dressed as a mouse tried to grab the feathers that were floating in the air. He bumped into a nearby table, and

tubs of paint and glue crashed to the ground.

The goblin dressed as a wolf hurried up to a girl holding a long blue ribbon. He took it right from her!

"Give that back!" the girl yelled. The ballroom quickly descended into noisy chaos as kids and goblins started to argue.

"Oh dear," whispered Gwen. "This is a disaster!"

Kirsty turned to Rachel. "We have to stop Jack Frost and his goblins before this gets any worse!"

Rachel nodded. The girls stood up—
and found themselves staring right into
the face of the mouse goblin.

"Hey, it's those girls!" the goblin
called out.

"Get them!" Jack Frost yelled.

Kirsty grabbed Rachel's hand.

"Run!" she cried.

Get That Pin!

The mouse goblin lunged for them and then tripped over a spilled bag of fuzzy pom-poms. The other three goblins charged after them from across the room.

"They're so fast!" Rachel cried, looking over her shoulder.

Kirsty quickly pulled her behind a big bin of fabric.

"But the goblins will find us here," Rachel said.

Kirsty grinned. "Not if we put on a disguise."

Rachel knew exactly what Kirsty was thinking. She grabbed a long piece of blue fabric. "Got it!" Rachel said.

The girls quickly wrapped the fabric around themselves. They wrapped it from their feet to their heads, leaving room for their eyes. They finished just as the goblins ran up.

Kirsty jumped up first.

"Aaaargh!" she cried. "We are the . . ."

". . . the blue mummies!" Rachel said,
jumping up next to her.

"Aaaah!" wailed the mouse goblin,
covering his eyes.

"Blue mummies!" yelled
the bear goblin.

"I want my
mommy!" cried
the wolf goblin.

"I don't remember
reading about blue
mummies in my
fairy tale book," the
cat goblin said. But
his friends were
already tugging him away
from the girls as fast as they could.

Rachel pulled the blue fabric away
from her face and grinned at Rachel. "It

worked!" she cried, unwinding the rest of
her costume.

Gwen fluttered up out of her pocket,
and hovered behind the fabric bin. "Good
job! Now, I think it's time I turned you
girls into fairies. Those goblins are sure
to be back any moment."

Kirsty and Rachel looked at each other
and smiled. They loved being turned into
fairies!

"Crouch down again, so no one will
see you," Gwen said. Then she waved
her wand.

The air glittered with fairy magic.
Tiny, sparkling roses with stems
appeared in the air. The glittering magic
surrounded Kirsty and Rachel. They
could feel themselves getting smaller as
tiny wings sprouted on their shoulders.

The girls fluttered
up to a large
chandelier
in the
center of
the room.
With all the
glitter and
feathers drifting

through the air, they knew no one would
notice them.

Below, they could see that the goblins
had returned to running around,
grabbing whatever items Jack Frost
needed. Most of the actual kids were
abandoning their costumes and leaving
the ballroom.

"Those kids in the animal costumes
are too mean!" one boy said.

Jack Frost didn't seem to care. He was busy cutting into some blue fabric with a pair of scissors.

"Ribbons, come to me!" he yelled to his goblins.

"He seems to be very interested in making that princess dress," said Gwen.

"Maybe he's concentrating so hard, he won't notice if we fly over and unhook the pin?" Kirsty asked.

"I'm not sure," Rachel said. "We'd be right underneath his pointy nose!"

"I'll distract him," Gwen said. "It won't be easy to unhook the pin. But your tiny fairy hands should do the trick."

"We'll do our best," Rachel promised.

"I'll fly in front of him first," said Gwen. "Then you two go for the pin."

Rachel and Kirsty nodded. The plan was in place!

Jack Frost was happily humming to himself as Gwen flew right in front of him.

"I am Beauty, yes that's me!" he sang.

"I know Beauty, and you are not her!" Gwen said.

Jack Frost looked up and scowled. "You! Get away from here. You're ruining my fairy tale!" he yelled.

Kirsty and Rachel started to flutter silently toward Jack Frost.

"This fairy tale doesn't belong to you. It belongs to everyone!" Gwen told him.

The girls hovered near Jack Frost's shoulder, just above the pin. So far, he was too busy arguing with Gwen to notice them.

Kirsty and Rachel each took a side of the magic rose pin.

"I see the clasp!" Rachel whispered.

"Gwen was right. Our fairy hands are just the size to open it," Kirsty said, and she reached for the clasp.

As she did, her wings fluttered against Jack Frost's shirt. He looked down. "Hey!" he cried. "Shoo! Get away!"

He swiped at them and the girls had to quickly fly out of the way to avoid being hit.

"Goblins!" he yelled.

The troop of goblins hurried toward him.

"Oh, no you don't!" Gwen said firmly. She pointed her magic wand at a container of paint. The paint covered the floor like an oil slick in front of the goblins.

Whomp! Whomp! Whomp! Whomp! The four goblins slipped and fell.

"No fair!" Jack Frost cried. Then he picked up a jar of glitter and poured it into his hand. He took a deep breath, and then he blew.

Whoosh! The glitter rained down
on Kirsty and Rachel as they tried to
fly away.

"Oh no!" Kirsty yelled. "It's making
my wings heavy!"

"We're falling!" Rachel cried.

"Hang on, girls!" Gwen called out,
flying after them.

But the girls were falling fast.

Kirsty tried to flap her wings, but they
wouldn't work. "We're going to hit the
floor!"

Then . . . *plop!* The girls
landed in something soft
and fuzzy.

Rachel sat
up, dazed.
"We're safe,"
she said.

"But what did we land in?" Kirsty asked, and then she looked up.

The soft, fuzzy face of the Beast was smiling down at them.

"Thanks, Beast!" Rachel said.

Two Beasts

Gwen flew up to the girls and hovered near Beast's giant paw.

"What a strange place this is," Beast said. "It doesn't look like my palace. I can't find Beauty anywhere. And it seems to be full of fairies!"

"Beast, we can help you get back to

your home," Rachel said. "But we need your help first!"

Beast frowned. "That man over there doesn't seem very nice."

"He's not!" said Kirsty. "He stole my friend Gwen's magic rose pin. And the book you gave to Beauty! We need to get it back from him."

"But how can I help?" Beast asked.

Rachel looked thoughtful. "I have an idea. Jack Frost wants to be the star of your fairy tale."

Beast looked surprised. "He does?"

"Yes!" said Kirsty. "He'll be thrilled to see you."

"And you can just ask him to give you the pin," Rachel said. "I bet he'll hand it right over, since you're the one asking!"

Beast stroked his hairy chin. "This is

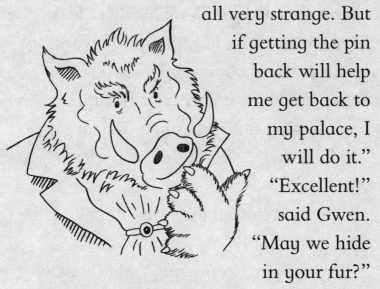

all very strange. But if getting the pin back will help me get back to my palace, I will do it."

"Excellent!" said Gwen. "May we hide in your fur?"

"Certainly!" Beast said. "Climb onto my back."

Kirsty and Rachel brushed the glitter off their wings. They flew up behind

Beast and landed next to Gwen. Then they grabbed onto his fur.

"Just use your beastly charm," Gwen told Beast.

"I will try," Beast said.

Beast headed to the table where Jack Frost stood all by himself, busily working on his princess costume. Rachel and Kirsty could see a corner of Beauty's book poking out from under the fabric.

"Hello there," Beast said in his deep voice.

Jack Frost looked up. "Beast!" he cried. "It's really you!"

"You seem to know me," said Beast. "But I do not know you."

"Of course you do," Jack Frost replied. "I am Beauty!"

Beast squinted his eyes. "*Hmm*. You don't look like Beauty."

"But I am!" Jack Frost insisted.

"If you were Beauty, then you would be wearing a special pin," said Beast. "It is shaped like a rose with a long stem."

Jack Frost got excited. "But I am wearing it!" He pointed to his shirt. "See? This proves I am Beauty."

"That doesn't look like a rose pin to me," said Beast.

Jack Frost stamped his foot. "It is! It is!"

"Can I please get a closer look at it?" Beast asked.

"Of course!" Jack Frost said.

Kirsty and Rachel held their breaths as Jack Frost unhooked the pin from his shirt. Then he placed it in Beast's furry paw.

Beast nodded. "Yes, that is the rose pin. And it's all yours, Gwen."

"Gwen? I'm not Gwen. I'm Beauty!" Jack Frost protested.

Gwen flew out from behind Beast's

head and touched the magic rose pin. It quickly shrank down to fairy size, and she pinned it onto her sweater, where it belonged.

"Noooooo!" Jack Frost wailed.

Just then, Beauty ran into the ballroom. "You!" she cried, pointing at Jack Frost. She marched right up to him and grabbed her magic book. "That is mine, thank you!"

"This is not fair!" Jack Frost complained. "Everybody's taking my stuff."

Beast leaned into Jack Frost's face. "It was never your stuff to begin with," he

growled. "Now I would suggest you get out of here, fast!"

Jack Frost turned pale. He slowly backed up, and then turned to run out of the ballroom, leaving a slight icy breeze in his wake.

"Well done!" Gwen cheered.

Kirsty and Rachel flew out from behind Beast.

"Thanks for all your help," Gwen told them. "And now I must turn you back into girls, so you can get ready for your party."

She waved her wand, and the sound of bells filled the air as the fairy magic did its work. Kirsty and Rachel were their normal selves again.

Gwen turned to Beauty and the Beast. "It's time to get you two back to your

fairy tale," she told them. Then she
turned to Kirsty and Rachel. "I'll be
back soon!" Gwen, Beauty, and Beast
vanished in a cloud of fairy dust.

"We helped save another fairy tale!"
Kirsty said.

Rachel grinned. "I'm glad Beauty and the Beast are back where they belong."

Then Amy, one of the festival organizers, popped her head into the ballroom.

"Wow, what a mess in here!" she said. "Have you girls finished your costumes yet? In a little while we need to start clearing things out for the party tonight."

"Um, we need a little more time," Rachel said quickly.

Amy nodded. "Okay. Good luck!" She closed the door, leaving the girls alone again.

Rachel and Kirsty looked at each other.

"What are we going to do?" Kirsty asked.

"We need to think of a fairy tale creature we can be," Rachel said. "What fairy tale creature is your favorite?"

Both girls smiled. "Beast!" they cried at the same time.

Creatures on Parade

"We'll need fur, and felt, and . . ."
Rachel stopped talking as she looked
around the ballroom. "Those goblins
made such a mess!"

"We'll never be able to find anything
we need!" Kirsty frowned.

Gwen suddenly reappeared in a
sparkling cloud of fairy dust. "I thought

you girls might need some help,"
she said.

She waved her wand, and fairy dust
and glittering roses rained down on the
ballroom. The costume supplies magically
returned to their boxes and bins. The
floor was sparkling clean again.

"Oh Gwen, thank you!" Rachel said.
She ran to a box of brown fake fur.
"This will be perfect for our Beast
costumes."

"You both are going as
Beast? How nice," Gwen
said. "He's my favorite
fairy tale creature,
of course."

She flew
over to the bin
of fur. "I can

whip up some wonderful Beast costumes for you with a wave of my wand," she offered.

"Thank you, but there are prizes for the best costumes, and that might be cheating," Kirsty said.

"But you can stay while we make our costumes," Rachel said. "I don't think it's cheating if you cheer us on."

Gwen smiled. "Of course not!" She nestled herself in a box of feathers as the ballroom doors opened, and other kids returned to finish their costumes.

The girls worked quickly to make their Beast outfits.

"We can make furry hoods to wear," Rachel said. "And glue felt ears on top."

"And make fancy vests out of felt that look like Beast's jacket!" Kirsty said.

"And wrap fur around our sleeves!" Rachel finished.

"I think your costumes are going to be wonderful," Gwen whispered.

Amy came back into the ballroom just as the girls were finishing. Gwen quickly ducked her head underneath the feathers so that Amy wouldn't see her.

"How did it go, Kirsty and Rachel?" Amy asked.

"We're all done," Rachel replied.

"Good!" Amy said. She turned to address everyone in the ballroom.

"It's almost time for dinner. Please take your costumes to your rooms. I can't wait to see what everyone's come up with!"

Amy left, and Gwen popped her head out of the box of feathers.

"Achoo!" she said. "I better head back to Fairyland now. Good luck tonight, girls!"

"Thank you!" the girls said, and Gwen disappeared in a shower of sparkles.

Later that night, the big clock in the main hall chimed seven

times. It was time for the Creature Costume Party!

The girls were proud of their matching costumes. They looked just like two miniature Beasts. They were amazed at how creative their fellow partygoers had been with their costumes, too. They couldn't believe their eyes as they made their way into the ballroom.

"Look, there's a unicorn!" Rachel said, pointing.

"And there's a frog! And a dragon!" Kirsty said.

They walked over to a table where a fountain of green punch sparkled under the ballroom lights.

"The goblins would have loved this!" Kirsty giggled.

Next to the punch bowl were plates

piled with cookies shaped like all kinds
of creatures. Rachel picked up one that
looked a little like Jack Frost.

"Take that!" she said, munching on it,
and Kirsty giggled again.

Then Amy stepped into the middle of
the ballroom, holding a microphone.

"What great costumes, everyone!" she
said. "Now it's time for the Creature

Parade! Please line up under the chandelier."

The girls ran to join the others in a line.

"Once around the ballroom!" Amy said.

The kids marched around the ballroom as music played. As they marched, Amy and two other festival organizers talked and made notes on everyone's outfits.

Then the music stopped.

"Wonderful!" said Amy. "And now it's time for prizes. Our first prize goes to Cutest Creature. And the winner is, Billy the Frog!"

The boy in the frog costume cheered and ran up to get his prize—a blue ribbon with a yellow medal that read, "Cutest Costume"!

Everyone cheered and clapped for Billy.

Then Amy announced the other prizes.
The girl dressed as a unicorn got the Most
Magical Costume. A girl in a dragon
costume won a prize for Best Scales.

"Do you think we'll win anything?"
Kirsty asked Rachel.

Then Amy called out the next prize.
"And the prize for Best Duo goes to Kirsty
and Rachel for their two mini Beasts!"

The girls ran up to Amy and she handed each of them a ribbon. Thrilled, they pinned the ribbons to the front of their felt vests.

After the rest of the prizes were given out, the music came back on and everyone danced in their creature costumes. By the time the party ended, both girls were very sleepy. Back in their room, they took off their costumes and scrubbed off their Beast noses.

Rachel picked up *The Fairies' Book of Fairy Tales*. Hannah the Happily Ever After Fairy had given it to them in Fairyland. The pages had all gone blank when Jack Frost stole the magic objects from the Fairy Tale Fairies.

Kirsty looked over Rachel's shoulder as Rachel flipped through the book. The

stories of Sleeping Beauty, Snow White, Cinderella, and The Frog Princess were all back in the book.

"And here's Beauty and the Beast!" said Rachel. "We helped save it."

Rachel flipped to the end of the book, where there were still many blank pages.

"And now we have two more fairy tales left to save!" Kirsty said.

THE FAIRY TALE FAIRIES

Rachel and Kirsty found Julia's, Eleanor's,
Faith's, Rita's, and Gwen's missing
magic objects. Now it's time for them to help

Aisha
the Princess and the Pea Fairy!

Join their next adventure in this
special sneak peek . . .

The Lost Princess

Kirsty and Rachel smiled at Aisha. She wore a cute, dark pink top with a matching flowy skirt. She had long black braids that fell past her shoulders. Her tiny, pink heeled shoes were decorated with black pom-poms.

"Aisha!" Kirsty cried. "It's so nice to see you again."

Rachel looked at the young woman in the doorway. "If you're here, that means that she—"

"Is the princess from *The Princess and the Pea*," finished Aisha.

The young woman frowned. "Princess? Pea?" she asked. Then she sighed. "I don't know what's wrong with me. I'm so confused!"

"You should come inside," Kirsty said quickly.

Aisha fluttered up to the princess. "You've lost your memory . . . sort of," she explained. "But don't worry, I'll help you, and so will my friends Kirsty and Rachel."

The princess nodded. "Thank you," she said, and then she shivered. "It's cold in here."

"We should get her some dry clothes," Rachel said. "I'm sure we could find something in her size in the costume closet."

Kirsty nodded and looked at Aisha. "Do you want to fly into my pocket? We have to make sure nobody sees you."

"Of course!" Aisha replied with a smile, and she flew into the front pocket of Kirsty's sweater.

Rachel turned to the princess. "Follow us."

RAINBOW magic™

Which Magical Fairies Have You Met?

- ☐ The Rainbow Fairies
- ☐ The Weather Fairies
- ☐ The Jewel Fairies
- ☐ The Pet Fairies
- ☐ The Dance Fairies
- ☐ The Music Fairies
- ☐ The Sports Fairies
- ☐ The Party Fairies
- ☐ The Ocean Fairies
- ☐ The Night Fairies
- ☐ The Magical Animal Fairies
- ☐ The Princess Fairies
- ☐ The Superstar Fairies
- ☐ The Fashion Fairies
- ☐ The Sugar & Spice Fairies
- ☐ The Earth Fairies
- ☐ The Magical Crafts Fairies
- ☐ The Baby Animal Rescue Fairies
- ☐ The Fairy Tale Fairies

■SCHOLASTIC

Find all of your favorite fairy friends at
scholastic.com/rainbowmagic

HIT entertainment

RMFAIRY